ONE
FINE
DAY
YOU'RE
GONNA
DIE

GAIL BOWEN

ONE FINE DAY YOU'RE GONNA DIE

RAVEN BOOKS
an imprint of
ORCA BOOK PUBLISHERS

Library and Archives Canada Cataloguing in Publication

Bowen, Gail, 1942-
One fine day you're gonna die / written by Gail Bowen.
(Rapid reads)

Issued also in an electronic format.
ISBN 978-1-55469-337-5

I. Title. II. Series: Rapid reads
PS8553.O8995O54 2010   C813'.54   C2010-903653-0

First published in the United States, 2010
Library of Congress Control Number: 2010929178

Summary: Events on Charlie D's radio show take a bizarre turn
when one of his callers threatens to kill not only himself
but also the young daughter of Charlie's on-air guest,
who happens to be an expert on death and dying. (RL 4.2)

Mixed Sources
Cert no. SW-COC-001271
© 1996 FSC
FSC

*Orca Book Publishers is dedicated to preserving the environment and has
printed this book on paper certified by the Forest Stewardship Council.*

Orca Book Publishers gratefully acknowledges the support for
its publishing programs provided by the following agencies:
the Government of Canada through the Canada Book Fund and the
Canada Council for the Arts, and the Province of British Columbia
through the BC Arts Council and the Book Publishing Tax Credit.

Design by Teresa Bubela
Cover photography by Getty Images

ORCA BOOK PUBLISHERS   ORCA BOOK PUBLISHERS
PO Box 5626, Stn. B   PO Box 468
Victoria, BC Canada   Custer, WA USA
V8R 6S4   98240-0468

www.orcabook.com
Printed and bound in Canada.

13 12 11 10 • 4 3 2 1

For everyone who reads this book

CHAPTER ONE

Tonight as I was riding my bike to the radio station where I do the late-night call-in show, a hearse ran a light and plowed into me. I swerved. The vehicle clipped my back wheel, and I flew through the air to safety. My Schwinn was not so lucky. The hearse skidded to a stop. The driver jumped out, sprinted over and knelt beside me on the wet pavement. "Are you all right?" he asked.

I checked my essentials.

"As all right as I'll ever be," I said.

The man bent closer. The streetlight illuminated both our faces. He looked like the actor who played Hawkeye on the old TV show *M*A*S*H*. His brow furrowed with concern when he saw my cheek.

"You're bleeding," he said.

"It's a birthmark," I said.

As birthmarks go, mine is a standout. It covers half my face, like a blood mask. Nine out of ten strangers turn away when they see it. This man moved in closer.

"The doctors weren't able to do anything?" he asked.

"Nope."

"But you've learned to live with it."

"Most of the time," I said.

"That's all any of us can do," the man said, and he grinned. His smile was like Hawkeye's—open and reassuring. He offered his hand and pulled me to my feet. "I'll take you wherever you want to go," he said.

He picked up my twisted Schwinn and stowed it in the back of the hearse. I slid into the passenger seat. The air inside was cool, flower-scented and oddly soothing. After we'd buckled our seat belts, the man turned the keys in the ignition.

"Where to?" he asked.

"CVOX Radio," I said. "728 Shuter."

"It's in a strip mall," he said. "Between a store that sells discount wedding dresses and a place that rents x-rated movies."

"I'm impressed," I said. "This is a big city."

"It is," he agreed. "But my business involves pick up and delivery. I need to know where people are."

Perhaps because the night was foggy and he'd already had one accident, the driver didn't talk as he threaded his way through the busy downtown streets. When we turned on to Shuter, I saw the neon call letters on the roof of our building. The *O* in CVOX ("ALL TALK/ALL THE TIME") is an open mouth with red lips and a tongue that looks like Mick Jagger's. Fog had fuzzed the brilliant scarlet neon of Mick's tongue to a soft pink. It looked like the kiss a woman leaves on a tissue when she blots her lipstick.

"I'll pick you up when your show's over," the man said.

"I'll take a cab," I said. "But thanks for the offer."

He shrugged and handed me a business card. "Call me if you change your mind. Otherwise, I'll courier a cheque to you tomorrow to pay for your bike."

"You don't know my name."

The man flashed me his Hawkeye smile. "Sure I do. Your name is Charlie Dowhanuik and you're the host of 'The World According to Charlie D.' I'm a fan. I even phoned in once. It was the night you walked off the show and disappeared for a year. You were in rough shape."

"That's why I left."

"I was relieved that you did," he said. "I sensed that if you didn't turn things around, you and I were destined to meet professionally. My profession, not yours. You were too young to need my services, so I called in to remind you of what Woody Allen said."

"I remember. 'Life is full of misery, loneliness and suffering and it's over much too soon.'" I met the man's eyes. "Wise words," I said. "I still ponder them."

"So you haven't stopped grieving for the woman you lost?"

"Nope."

"But you decided to keep on living," he said.

"For the time being," I said. We shook hands, and I opened the car door and climbed out. As I watched the hearse disappear into the fog, the opening lines of an old schoolyard rhyme floated to the top of my consciousness.

Do you ever think when a hearse goes by
That one fine day you're gonna die?
They'll wrap you up in a cotton sheet
And throw you down about forty feet.
The worms crawl in,
The worms crawl out...

There was more, but I had to cut short my reverie. It was October 31. Halloween. The Day of the Dead. And I had a show to do.

CHAPTER TWO

Late at night, Studio D is a fine and private place. The CVOX offices are empty, and except for the security guy and a technician down the hall, our show's producer, Nova Langenegger, and I are on our own. After ten years of working together, Nova and I know each other's moods, and we anticipate one another's needs.

Tonight Nova anticipates that I need a guest expert on death and grieving to keep me from going into freefall during the show. Halloween is tough for me. I met Ariel, the woman I loved and lost, at a Halloween birthday party. We were seven years old. She was dressed as the sun, and the memory of her shining face surrounded by rays of golden foil still stops my heart.

Nova is not often wrong, but as soon as I walk into the control room of Studio D, I know that we're in for a rocky ride. The guest expert and my producer are standing toe to toe, and they both look grim. A stranger who didn't know the combatants would put his money on the guest expert.

Dr. Robin Harris is a goddess. In her stilettos, she's taller than me, and I'm an even six feet. Her skin is creamy; her eyes are green; her auburn hair falls in luxuriant waves over her shoulders. Her black leather coat is close-fitted to showcase her many assets.

At my request, Nova is wearing the caterpillar costume that she'd worn to a party earlier in the evening. Her six-month-old daughter, Lily, had been dressed as a butterfly. On a good day, Nova ticks in at a little over five foot two. In my opinion she's a beauty, but these days she's haunted by the few extra pounds she picked up when she was pregnant.

The tension in the control room is thick, and the body language is hostile. I attempt to defuse the situation.

"Dr. Harris, I presume." I offer our guest my hand. "I'm Charlie Dowhanuik."

Dr. Harris pivots on her stilettos. She ignores my outstretched hand. Her eyes are flashing. "I've asked your producer to block a certain caller, and she refuses." Dr. Harris's voice is the kind of deep rich mezzo that makes my knees weak, but the caterpillar and I have a history.

"We don't block callers unless there's a reason," I say.

"There's a reason," Robin Harris says. "Dr. Gabriel Ireland and I were in a relationship. It's over, and he's not dealing with it well. He makes threats."

"Against you?" I say.

Robin Harris shakes her head impatiently. "Against himself," she says. "He threatens to commit suicide."

"In that case, he shouldn't be ignored," I say. "Maybe I can help."

Robin Harris's thrilling voice drips contempt. "I doubt it," she says.

Nova catches my eye and points to the darkened studio on the other side of the glass.

"You'd better get in there," she says. "We're on air in one minute, five."

I open the door to the studio and stand aside for Dr. Harris. As she glides past me, I catch her perfume. It's sultry. We take our places at the round broadcast desk. I point to her earphones.

"Those are yours. Could you say a few words, please? Nova needs to do a sound check."

Dr. Harris flicks the button on the base of her microphone and the tiny light indicating that she's on the air comes to life.

"If you don't block Dr. Gabriel Ireland's calls, you'll regret it," she says.

I raise an eyebrow.

"On-air tension is the lifeblood of talk radio," I say.

As she hears Dr. Harris's words, Nova's smile is sweet. When we're on the air, Nova and I communicate through hand signals and our talkback microphone. Unless Nova chooses to open the talkback for the guest, I'm the only one who can hear her. Tonight she's decided not to share with Dr. Harris. Nova's voice on the talkback is amused.

"FYI, Charlie, Dr. Harris tells me that people from an unnamed network are listening to our show tonight. Dr. Harris is on the short list for a call-in show of her own. My guess is she doesn't want Gabriel

Ireland getting through because he might put her off her game."

"O-kay," I say.

"There's an introduction on your computer screen," Nova says. She holds up five fingers and counts down. "And you're on the air."

Our theme music, "Ants Marching" by the Dave Matthews Band, comes up. When the music fades, it's my turn. Like everyone in my business, I've created a voice that works for my audience. My radio voice is soothing, deep and intimate, but tonight I take it down a few notches and open with the sepulchral tones of the villain in a horror movie.

"Good evening. I'm Charlie Dowhanuik and you are listening to 'The World According to Charlie D.' It's October thirty-first, the Day of the Dead, and our topic is—DEATH! How do you see it? A bony guy carrying a scythe rasping out your name, or a heavenly

choir robed in white calling you home? Do you fear it? Do you welcome it? What do you think about the way we, as a society, handle death? Where do you stand on funerals— do you want to be torched and scattered to the four winds, or do you want the full meal deal with incense, prayers and all the bells and whistles. Our lines are open. Give me a call at 1-800-555-2333 or email me at charlie d at nation tv dot com.

"I'm joined tonight by Dr. Robin Harris, medical doctor, sociologist and expert in the arts of dying and grieving. Welcome, Dr. Harris."

"Thank you for inviting me, Charlie D." The warmth and fullness of her voice are extraordinary. The network guys for whom she's auditioning must be creaming their jeans. She adjusts her notes. *"The questions you raise are complex, and as a thanatologist, I believe I can contribute specialized knowledge that will be helpful to your listeners."*

"We're in your debt," I say. "Now tell me, in words that make sense to us all, what exactly does a thanatologist do?"

"In words that make sense to your audience, I study how people in varying cultures at varying times have dealt with death. I believe there are lessons there that can help people on the most vulnerable days of their lives."

"And those days would be…?"

"The day when they themselves are about to die or when they learn that someone significant in their life has died."

I remember the exact moment when I heard that my golden, glowing Ariel had died. She was twenty-eight years old. When she was thirteen, she made a tablecloth out of midnight blue velvet and appliquéd it with gold and silver satin cut-outs of suns, moons, stars, buds, blossoms, fruits, birds, fish and animals. Ariel's world encompassed everything, and then she was gone. We used the cloth she sewed to cover the box that held her ashes. Suddenly I can't speak. Through the glass that separates us, I see Nova's worried eyes and the quarter smile that she offers when I need encouragement.

CHAPTER THREE

On talk radio, dead air is the enemy. Spotting her chance, Doctor Harris leans in to her microphone. People from the unnamed network are listening, assessing how Dr. Harris can handle situations on air. But people for whom I am a lifeline are also listening. I failed them once before. I'm not going to let it happen again. I dig deep for my cool and commanding voice, and it's there.

"So you deal with people who are about to die or people who've just lost someone they love," I say. *"Heavy stuff."*

Dr. Harris's laugh is warm and self-deprecating.

"Heavy stuff indeed, but I teach people how to do the heavy lifting."

"You make it sound so easy—like doing push-ups."

"Handling death is like doing push-ups," she says smoothly. *"At first you think you can't get past your weakness, but if you persist, every day you get stronger. You simply have to show your grief that you're its master."*

Everything about Robin Harris is without flaw. Her profile is classic; the lines of her neck are graceful; the deep plum polish on the perfect ovals of her fingernails matches the gloss on her lips. As she utters her insights, her voice is certain. I think of my listeners, broken and vulnerable, and of me, broken and vulnerable too.

"Where were you when I needed you?" I say.

Her green eyes meet mine.

"You lost someone?"

"Yup."

"And...?"

"And...I'll never touch her body again, or smell the fragrance of her skin or hear her voice. I'm like Eurydice in the underworld when she stretches out her arms to Orpheus, struggling to be grasped and to grasp him..." My voice breaks.

Nova's voice comes through the talkback.

"Want me to go to music?"

I shake my head.

"And catches fleeting air," Dr. Harris says. *"I'm familiar with the story. Incidentally, Orpheus didn't have to lose Eurydice. He could have carried her back from the underworld if he'd honored his promise not to look at her."*

"His fault," I say.

"Most of our suffering is self-induced," Dr. Harris says coolly. *"We have to be strong enough to face that. And move on."*

"That would be a trick," I say. *"I'm sure Orpheus would have benefited from your counsel, Dr. Harris—I'm sure you would have saved the day."*

Nova runs a finger across her throat, indicating that I should stick a sock in it.

"I'm going to music," she says through the talkback. "Info's on your computer screen. Then we'll take a caller." She pauses. "Don't let her draw you in, Charlie. We'll get through this. Lunch tomorrow is on me."

I read Nova's notes announcing "Manhã de Carnaval" from *Black Orpheus*. The music comes up and I meet Dr. Harris's eyes. "This is certainly going well," I say.

"I don't like your tone," she says.

"Neither do I," I say. "Unfortunately, it's the only tone I have."

I open the talkback, so I'm certain Nova hears the conversation. "Dr. Harris, why don't you and I park our egos and get on with this? When you have your own show—and I'm sure you will—the spotlight will be on you. 'The World According to Charlie D' focuses on our callers. You and I got off to a bad start tonight. Let's just chill and listen to the music. When it's over, we'll start taking calls. Any questions?"

"None that you could answer," she says. The melody has gone from her voice.

Until the music ends, Dr. Harris shuffles through her notes, and I watch her shuffle. We're like two people on the world's worst blind date. Nova peers at us over her wire-rimmed reading glasses and bites her nails. She's a committed nail-chewer and, lovely as she is, her hands look like a nervous six-year-old's. "And we're back," she says finally.

I turn on my microphone. *"That was 'Manhã de Carnaval' from the original sound track for the film* Black Orpheus. *I'm Charlie Dowhanuik, and you are listening to 'The*

World According to Charlie D.' Our topic on this Halloween night is the big D. Death. So how do you see 'being defunct'? One of these days all of us will head for the last roundup. Yippee ai oh kay ay. Are you ready to saddle up? Made your will? Filled out your donor card? Made peace with your enemies? Made peace with yourself? Give us a call at 1-800-555-2333. Let us know what you've done to prepare for the moment when you shake hands with Mr. Death.

"And for those of you who've just joined us, we have a guest tonight. Dr. Robin Harris is a thanatologist, a specialist who knows everything there is to know about death and dying. Dr. Harris is 'professionally equipped' to advise the rest of us on how to face our fears when the Grim Reaper taps on our imagination.

"Our first caller is Louise, from Sudbury. Greetings, Louise, what's on your mind tonight?"

Words can lie but voices never do. Louise has the rasp of a woman who has enjoyed her whiskey, her cigarettes and her men. I like her.

"Hi, Charlie D," she says. *"And hello, Dr. Robin...sorry, I didn't catch your last name. Anyway, what's on my mind tonight is my mother."* Louise chortles. *"Dead or alive, it's always about her."*

"So I take it your mother is no longer with us," I say.

"You take it correctly, and I want to talk about how pissed I am at the way she died."

Our guest expert adjusts her mike.

"Louise, this is Dr. Robin Harris." She articulates her name with the care of someone attempting to teach a cow to speak. *"So you're calling because your mother suffered greatly,"* she says.

Louise is huffy.

"She didn't suffer at all, Dr. Robin Harris. My mother was ninety-two years old and she died in her own bed with clean sheets, her own

teeth, a silk nightie with the price tag still on it, and a smile on her face a mile wide."

"There's something you're reluctant to share," Dr. Harris says.

"I'm not reluctant. You just motored in before I had a chance to finish."

Our guest expert raises a perfectly arched eyebrow.

"Something about your mother's death distresses you," she says.

Louise is a plainspoken woman with little patience for pretty words.

"It doesn't 'distress' me, Dr. Robin Harris. It pisses me off. As I was saying, I made sure Mother was clean and sprayed down with Elizabeth Taylor's White Diamonds; then I gave her permission to die. I used the exact words Oprah said to use. 'Mother,' I said. 'Your work here is done. It's okay for you to leave. I'll be fine.' After that, Mother's eyes got misty and she raised her old arms and said, 'I'm coming, Andrew.'" ·

Robin Harris finds the low, smoldering notes of her magnificent voice.

"And you were hurt that at the end of her life, your mother didn't reach out to you. She reached out to your father."

Louise's exasperation reaches the boiling point and spills over.

"Doctor, I may not have degrees up the wazoo the way you do, but I know how to listen. My father's name was Walter. Andrew was the name of the angel on that cheesy TV show, Touched By an Angel. *You can catch it in reruns. Mother never missed an episode. Anyway, I'm sitting there bawling my eyes out, and there's Mother on her deathbed, reaching out to this actor who is now doing a commercial for cat food."*

"And you want to know how to deal with your anger toward your mother?" Robin says.

Louise's laugh is infectious.

"I'm not angry at Mother. I just wanted to get that off my chest, and now I have.

Jeez, Touched By an Angel. *Thanks for being there, Charlie D. Dr. Robin Harris, I hope you learn a little something tonight about how to listen to people."*

Louise's imitation of our guest's precise enunciation of her own name is deadly. As I take the next call, I see the pulse in Dr. Harris's white throat throbbing with anger. It's going to be a long night.

CHAPTER FOUR

For a person with an extraordinary gift for using her own voice, Dr. Harris seems remarkably tone-deaf when it comes to the voices of others. Our next caller is Garnet from Saskatoon. He wants to talk about respecting the dignity of the dead. He'd been at a friend's funeral the week before. The man was estranged from his family, and his ex-wife had arranged for an open-casket funeral with her ex-husband lying in state wearing his Ray-Bans. When Dr. Harris rattles on about King Tut being buried with golden chariots and a fleet of miniature ships, Garnet sniffs that she seems to have a special talent for missing the point. The good doctor is two for two.

Louise and Garnet were strong enough to deal with Robin Harris's empathy challenges. Our next caller won't be. Danny is a sixteen-year-old boy who was in a car accident at the beginning of the summer. He was driving, and his brother was killed.

Over the talkback, Nova warns me that because Danny is fragile, I must keep Robin Harris in check. There's another cloud on the horizon. The caller following Danny is Dr. Gabriel Ireland. Today is his fortieth birthday, and it's not shaping up to be a good one. Nova has decided against blocking his call.

Danny has agreed to let me paint the broad strokes of his situation for our listeners. I explain Danny's role in the death of his brother and his fear that he will never feel normal again. Then I turn it over to him. Danny waits a beat too long to begin, and Dr. Harris pounces.

"You wonder if you'll ever feel normal again, Danny," she says. *"Each grief has its own rhythm. In time you'll…"*

I cut her off. *"Why don't we let Danny tell us how he's feeling?"*

Danny is painful to listen to. He announces his problem right away.

"I stutter," he says. *"I didn't use to, but s…s…since the accident…I…I…I…Charlie D, I can't do this…"*

"Sure you can," I say. *"Just imagine that you and I are—where's your favorite place in the world?"*

As I wait for Danny to answer, I watch the second hand on the studio clock measure the silence. Thirty-five seconds of dead air—an eternity in talk radio, but Danny comes through.

"The dock at our cottage," he says finally.

"Okay, good," I say. "Imagine that we're sitting on the dock at your cottage—just the two of us—and you're telling me that since the accident..."

His stutter makes listening to Danny's story difficult, but he soldiers on.

"Since the accident, it's like there's a plug in my throat, and all my words get stuck. I can't say what I want to say."

"What do you want to say?"

"I hate that Liam's dead. I hate that it's my fault."

"Accidents are no one's fault," I say. "They can happen to anyone."

"That's what everyone keeps telling me. But it happened to me because...because... because..." Danny's voice is thick with despair. "I can't say the words, Charlie D..."

"Danny, take a deep breath. Close your eyes. We're on the dock—just you and me—shootin' the breeze. Why did the accident happen to you?"

"*Because...because...*" Suddenly the logjam is broken. The words pour out. "*Because I loved Liam, but sometimes I wanted him to go away. He was smarter at school. He was a better runner than me. He didn't have zits. Everybody liked him best...even my Dad.*"

Dr. Robin Harris leans in to her mike.

"*Rivalries between brothers are natural. Starting with Cain and Abel...*"

Danny has finally opened up. To be cut off just as he's found his voice reduces him to tears.

"*I don't know who Cain and that other guy are,*" he says. "*This is about me and Liam. Can I just talk to Charlie D? Please. I just want to talk to Charlie D. Why doesn't anything ever work for me?*"

"*We can make it work,*" I say. "*Stay on the line. My producer, Nova, will get your number. As soon as the show's off the air, I'll call you. We can talk for as long as you want. Off air. Just us. Okay?*"

"Okay."

"Good man. Later?"

"Later."

I glance at the control room. Nova has the phone tucked between her ear and her shoulder, and she's keying information into her computer. I glance at my computer screen. Danny's contact info is there. So is a single sentence. Sometimes we do good work. I look through the glass into the control room. When I catch her eye, Nova gives me the thumbs-up.

"Time to regroup," I say. *"What tunes do you want played at your send-off? Some groups seem like naturals. The Grateful Dead? Undertakin' Daddies? Cold Play? Choose carefully. Remember, you don't get a second chance to make a last request. Give us a call at 1-800-555-2333."*

Robin Harris is clearly not in the mood for fun and games, but I am conciliatory.

"Dr. Harris, what's your pleasure?"

Her brilliant green eyes shoot daggers.

"*Verdi's* Requiem," she says.

"*Ah, music as stately and regal as you are,*" I say. "*A perfect choice, but I suspect all your choices are perfect.*"

"*I believe in a well-ordered life,*" she says; then, suddenly mindful of the network executives who've tuned in to catch her act, she offers an on-air olive branch. "*What about you, Charlie D? What do you want played at your funeral?*"

"Something tasty," I say. "*Maybe 'Deep as Love' by the Tord Gustavsen Trio. Let's set a spell and listen.*"

Tord's trio is soothing. Nova's words over the talkback are not. "Dr. Gabriel Ireland is up next," she says. "Charlie, I struggled with this one. We may just be getting dragged into an ugly game between Gabe and Dr. Harris, but I've been talking to Gabe. He's going down for the third time. I don't think we have a choice. If Dr. Harris gives you any static, tell her this is my decision. She can beat me up after the show."

"Nope," I say. "All decisions around here are arrived at jointly. If you get beat up, I get beat up. But stand in front of me. That caterpillar costume you're wearing appears to be bulletproof."

Nova gives me her crooked smile, and immediately I feel better.

CHAPTER FIVE

Tord's piano is sweet and tuneful, but Dr. Harris is not placated. "You don't have the training to handle an adolescent as disturbed as Danny," she says. "He needs a specialist." She turns her face toward the control room to allow me to absorb her words. Her profile is classical, perfect and distant.

Without exchanging a single word with Gabriel Ireland, I can understand why he is crazy in love with this woman. Luckily for me, I have never been drawn to ice queens.

"Danny didn't call a specialist," I say. "He called me. Dr. Harris, we have a database with referral numbers for professionals in every area where we're heard. When we have a caller whose problems demand the kind of help I can't give them, I talk to them after the show and I refer them to a professional. I'm just Step One."

"You're the wrong step," she says crisply. "As long as you operate within your area of expertise, you're amusing. But you're out of your depth with someone as seriously disturbed as Danny. For him, this could be a matter of life and death."

Dr. Harris's condescension raises my hackles.

"That's precisely the reason why I cut you off," I say. "As Louise noted so colorfully, you have degrees up the wazoo, but what you did with Danny was just plain stupid. That boy is being eaten alive by guilt because he wanted his brother dead

35

and he got his wish. But instead of letting Danny say the words he needs to say if he's ever going to recover, you launch into a lecture about Cain and freaking Abel."

"Pointing out to Danny that his feelings are archetypal is accepted clinical protocol."

"He's sixteen years old, and he's disintegrating. He doesn't need to hear about archetypes. He just needs someone to listen. By the way, Dr. Harris, we're back on the air in ten, and get ready, because I'm going to give you a chance to strut your stuff."

"And we're back," I say. *"Judging by the number of calls coming in on this, the Day of the Dead, a lot of you are haunted by ghoulies, ghosties, long-leggedy beasties and things that go bump in the night. Luckily we have a pro to help us battle the ghoulies and ghosties. Tonight, I'm joined by Dr. Robin Harris, a thanatologist, a specialist in death. Dr. Harris, how did you get into your line of work?"*

"For me, thanatology has always been a journey in search of answers," she says in her thrilling voice. *"When I was seven, my grandmother died. My parents had pretty much abandoned me, but my grandmother had always been there. I was alone with her when she had her fatal heart attack."*

"That must have been terrifying."

"It was," Robin agrees. *"But my grandmother always told me that whatever didn't kill me would make me stronger. I realize now she was just repeating a truism, but I clung to those words. I was determined not to let my grandmother's death kill me, and so I began to think seriously about what death meant. Even as a child, I knew that death was a natural phenomenon. I'd seen dead birds. I'd had pets that died. The principal of my school fell down a flight of stairs and broke her neck. Death was all around, so I made a decision to understand what it meant."*

"That was pretty gutsy," I say.

Glowing with the sheen of self-love, Robin continues her autobiography.

"It was necessary," she says. *"I was a logical child, so I set out to find answers. After my grandmother died, I went to live with my mother's brother and his wife. As fate would have it, my uncle owned a funeral home, and I spent hours with him, listening to his stories about how people reacted to death."*

"And you were seven years old," I say.

"I wasn't afraid," she says. *"My uncle recognized a kindred spirit in me. He told me that I'd been given a great gift. I was able to observe grief without being affected."*

"That's quite a trick."

"There's no trick to it. Knowledge is power."

"So your knowledge of death gives you power over it?"

"Yes."

"And the fact that you're not afraid of death gives you power over people who are."

"That's a little simplistic, but yes."

I shake my head.

"Whoa! Lady Death, you are a trip. Time to talk to a caller. Here's one that should interest you. It's from a friend of your daughter."

Robin laughs.

"My daughter is six years old. Her friends are all in bed by now."

Gabriel Ireland's pleasant tenor voice is ironic and resigned. I recognize the tone. This is a man who has nothing more to lose.

"Not all your daughter's friends are six years old, Robin. Kali tells me I'm her best friend, and as you well know, my dark star, today is my fortieth birthday. Since you've sucked the light out of every moment of my last year, it seems only fitting that I spend these last dark minutes with you."

Robin shakes her head in disgust, but I jump in.

"Gabe, our show is pretty loose, but we have two rules: no straying from the topic and

no hitting below the belt. So far you're two for two."

"I apologize," Gabriel Ireland says, and he sounds genuinely contrite. *"I'm a hollow man."*

"You're a bore," Robin Harris says sharply. *"Gabe, hang up and let someone with real problems call in. I'm not here to deal with your adolescent angst."*

"I'm aware of that, my dark star. I've been listening. As always, you established the boundaries brilliantly. You said your job is to help people deal with the day in their lives when they are most vulnerable—the day when they're about to die or when someone they love is about to die. I qualify on both counts."

CHAPTER SIX

Robin flicks off her microphone. Her creamy skin is blotched with anger. "I told your producer this would happen if she put his call through. Gabe is hijacking your show, and he's making me look bad." Her eyes meet mine. "It's either Gabe or me," she says. "Cut him off or I leave."

Nova's voice on the talkback is tight. "Stay with Gabe, Charlie. I know voices, and Gabriel Ireland is in real trouble. We have a caller named Boomer on line two. He thinks he can help. At the very least, he'll give everybody a chance to take a deep breath."

I shrug. What the hell? It's Halloween— the night for trick or treat. I switch my mike on.

"Gabe, why don't we chill awhile and listen to what another caller has to say."

Gabe laughs.

"I'm not going anywhere, Charlie."

Robin takes off her headphones and starts jamming her notes into her briefcase. I give her an apologetic smile, open line two and glance at my computer screen.

"Good evening, Boomer." I say. *"I see that you identify your hometown as wherever your Harley will take you. So are you on the road now?"*

"Nope, getting too old to drive in the dark."

Boomer's rumbling bass makes me reach for the volume control.

"My pattern now," he says, *"is to ride the Hog until sundown, pull into a motel,*

crack open a cool one and wait until you come on the air."

"Proud to be part of your day," I say.

"Thanks, Charlie D. Anyway, I just wanted to let Gabe know that I had a dark star of my own. I was with this lady for two years, and it was stellar—especially in the dark. This lady and I were cut from the same cloth. We both loved to ride our Harleys. We both loved the band Pantera and the Meatlovers Pan-Scrambler at Humpty's. Most of all, we loved taking long showers together. There was a little place on my lady's back that she couldn't reach, and she liked me to soap the spot with Zest. She and I had a lot of fine moments, but there was something about the smell of Zest on that woman that was so good it made me cry."

Robin has put on her coat and is knotting her scarf. It appears that my apologetic smile has lost its charm.

I keep my focus on Boomer.

"I know the feeling," I say.

"*I kind of figured you did,*" Boomer says. "*Anyway, long story short, my lady found a biker with a bigger Hog, and she moved along. For a long time, I was kind of where Gabe is now. After my lady left, I soaped a lot of backs, but none of them passed the Zest test. I was beginning to think I'd lost something I would never find again, then along came a lady with a bar of Dove.*"

"*And soaping your new lady with Dove was good?*"

"*Transcendent,*" Boomer booms.

I wouldn't have figured Boomer as a guy who'd describe his love life as "transcendent," but life is full of surprises.

"*So your message to Gabe is that somewhere there's a lady with a bar of Dove that has his name on it?*"

"*You got it, Charlie D.*" Boomer's laughter is as generous and enveloping as a bear hug.

"Thanks for calling," I say, and I mean it. The light on line two goes out, and I'm back to line one.

"So, Gabe, think you can hang on until your Cinderella appears?"

"I've pretty much given up on happily-ever-afters," Gabe says. *"When my radio came on this morning and I heard the announcer say that Robin was going to be your guest, I saw the shape of my day. I'd drive to the hospital, listen to jokes from my colleagues about turning forty, open a couple of gag gifts and pretend to be surprised when someone brought a cafeteria cake into the staff lounge. And that would be my birthday. At the end of my shift, I'd go back to an empty condo and life without Robin and Kali. I couldn't face it."*

Robin levels a last lethal look at me and walks out the studio door. She doesn't wave goodbye.

I turn my attention back to Gabe.

"*So you decided to call in to our show tonight,*" I say.

"*Only after picking up the one thing I needed to make my birthday complete,*" he says.

My heart is pounding.

"*And what was that?*" I ask.

"*A vial of saxitoxin.*"

Robin has entered the control room. The space is brightly lit. I see everything, but hear nothing. It's like watching a silent movie. Without even a glance at Nova, Robin strides through the door that leads to the hall that will take her out of CVOX.

I open the talkback to Nova.

"We can't lose Robin," I say. "Go after her. Unless I'm mistaken, Gabe is playing for keeps. Tell Robin that if she saves Gabe's life on air, she'll be able to write her own ticket for her call-in show."

When the control-room door closes behind Nova, my pulse begins to race.

It's just me and Gabe now. I turn on my microphone.

"Okay, Gabe. You've got my attention. What's saxitoxin?"

CHAPTER SEVEN

G abe is clinical. *"Saxitoxin is a poison,"* he says. There is no hint of emotion in his pleasant tenor. He might be delivering a lecture or reading an entry from a text-book. *"Some people call it shellfish toxin,"* he says. *"It kills quickly. And there's no antidote."*

"So if a person changes his or her mind, nothing can be done," I say.

I stare at the door that separates the CVOX control room from the world where no one can control anything. Gabe continues his lecture about saxitoxin. The seconds tick by on the studio clock.

No one comes through the door to the control room. Nova is smart and persuasive, but Robin's egotism may be a rock that cannot be cracked.

Just when I reconcile myself to flying solo, the door opens. As she resumes her customary place on the other side of the glass, Nova gives me a discreet thumbs-up. Robin sweeps back into the studio, takes her chair and slips on her earphones. She listens long enough to hear Gabe say that death from an injection is painless, and then she turns on her microphone and pounces.

"Gabe, you're not interested in injecting yourself with anything. You're not interested in dying. You're just interested in making my life a living hell."

"If your life is a living hell, why not join me?" Gabe says. *"The vial is full. Saxitoxin for all."*

Robin shrugs off her coat. Seemingly she's back on the team.

I turn off my mike and switch on the talkback. Nova is tense, but she's in command. "Get Gabe's address from Dr. Harris and keep him talking until we can get a police shrink there."

"Will do," I say. "Dr. H., what's Gabe's home address?"

Robin's face flushes with anger. She reaches over and flicks on her microphone.

"Gabe, listen to me. You've got everyone here in a panic, but I know you're faking. Don't play along, Charlie D."

I attempt to clear the air. *"Gabe, this is a high-stakes game, so I need you to tell me the truth. Are you planning to commit suicide?"*

"I prefer to think of it as exiting on my own terms," he says.

There's a hopelessness in his voice that I recognize.

"Let's rethink this, Gabe," I say. *"I've been where you are, standing so close to the Gate of Hell I could read the inscription over the entrance."*

"'Abandon all hope, ye who enter here.'" Gabe supplies the passage from Dante's *Inferno.* "*One of life's nastier surprises is that even our suffering is not unique.*"

Dr. Harris cannot contain her impatience.

"Gabe, you're an adult. Whether you choose to end your life is your decision. I've lost track of the number of times you've threatened suicide. You're like the boy who cried wolf."

"Ah, but one day, there really was a wolf, and he ate the boy. My wolf is a vial of saxitoxin. It takes so little—there's more than enough here for both of us. Just a pinprick from the hypodermic and, within seconds, oblivion. Would you like to say goodbye, my dark star?"

Robin spits out her response.

"To you? I don't think so. I've already said goodbye to you a hundred times. You never get the message."

Gabe sounds weary.

"Actually, I was wondering if you'd like to say goodbye to your daughter."

"*What?*" For the first time since she walked into the studio, cracks appear in Robin Harris's facade. "*What are you talking about, Gabe?*"

"*You never quite hear me, do you, my dark star? I simply asked if you wanted to say goodbye to Kali?*"

Robin's eyes are wide with fear.

"*What are you talking about? You know I wouldn't let you anywhere near my daughter.*"

"*Too late, Robin. She's here with me now.*"

"*You're lying. I talked to Kali two hours ago. Her nanny had just given her a bath and tucked her in.*"

"*And Kali was wearing her new pajamas— the ones I bought her for Halloween—but why don't I let Kali tell you about them.*"

As she describes her new pajamas, Kali's voice is as tuneful as a well-played flute.

"*You were gone before Gabe came, Mummy. The pajamas he gave me are dark blue and they're covered in moons and stars...and when*" *the lights go out, the moons and stars glow in the dark."*

Dr. Robin Harris seems to crumple before me.

"That's her voice," she says. "Oh my god, Gabe has my daughter."

CHAPTER EIGHT

For the first seconds after she hears that her six-year-old is with Gabe, Dr. Harris looks as if she's been sucker-punched. But she's a champ, and she comes out swinging. She pulls her microphone closer, a rookie mistake but—given the circumstances—understandable. I reach over and adjust it.

"How did you get her, Gabe?" she asks. She makes no attempt to disguise the hostility in her voice. Both Robin's tone and her question surprise me. I thought her first concern would be Kali's safety. But it's not.

Dr. Harris obviously sees Gabe's possession of her daughter as a kind of power play.

"What did you promise Inge?" she asks. *"She would never simply hand Kali over to you. She's been my nanny since Kali was born."*

"Which means she has seen how deeply I love you both," Gabe says quietly. *"Inge and I talk all the time. She's been concerned about this rift between you and me. I wish you could have seen her face when I told her the estrangement was over."*

"She believed you?" Robin says.

"She was ecstatic," Gabe says. *"We were all ecstatic, weren't we, Kali? Kali and I were so happy that we decided to let Inge go to a Halloween party she was invited to and have an adventure of our own."*

"Gabe, I need to talk to my daughter."

"When you're angry, all the music goes from your voice, Robin. Mummy's a little upset, Kali. You can say hi to her, but remember we can't tell her where we are. That's a secret."

"Hi, Mummy," Kali says. She is at the center of this drama, but her voice is bubbly and unconcerned. *"Gabe bought me a new game of Candy Land. We played it up at the lake, 'member?"*

Robin's tone is urgent.

"Listen to me, Kali. You have to get away from Gabe. Start screaming and run."

There's a bell-like sound in the background on Gabe's end of the line. I raise a finger and mouth the word *listen* to Robin. She furrows her brow in concentration but shakes her head. She can't identify what we're hearing.

Gabe comes back on the line.

"My turn to talk, Kali," he says. *"Mummy doesn't understand that we're playing two games tonight. You and I are playing Candy Land, and all of us are playing hide and seek. Mummy is It. It's not fair for the person who's It to tell us to scream and run, because as soon as she finds us, the game is over."*

Robin's composure shatters.

"Gabe, please..."

"Your voice is full of music again," Gabe says. *"I've never been able to resist your music. Kali wants us to sing a song for you. I want to do that too. We want you to remember how much we loved you."*

Suddenly I know this isn't a game. This is for real.

"Gabe, you're not going to—"

He cuts me off. *"Kali, let's sing for Mummy."*

Gabe's voice is a pleasant tenor, and Kali's little girl voice is fresh and tuneful. They sing a duet: "You Are My Sunshine." By the time they finish, Nova is in tears, and my throat is thick. Robin is frantic.

"Kali, listen to me," she says. *"This isn't a game. Gabe isn't your friend. He's going to hurt you. You have to get away."*

"She can't hear you, Robin," Gabe says. *"I have the phone, and you won't be talking*

to Kali anymore because you cheat. You don't play by the rules. I'm not surprised but I am disappointed. I had hoped that perhaps since this was the last time the three of us would be together..."

My heart is pounding. I can barely form the words.

"Gabe, don't kill that little girl."

"Trust me, Charlie," he says gently. *"It's for the best."*

"How can killing a six-year-old child be 'for the best'?"

Gabe sounds very tired. *"There are circumstances..."*

I find myself shouting.

"What circumstances could possibly justify taking a child's life?"

"There aren't any." Robin's voice is fervent. *"Gabe, stop this. I want my daughter. I won't press charges. I give you my word."*

"Even the music in your voice won't sway me this time, my dark star. There've been

too many words, and I remember them all—especially the ones at the end. You told me I 'no longer meet your needs.' I wept, but your eyes, 'those silent tongues of love' Cervantes wrote about, were cold. You were my whole existence, Robin."

"People fall out of love," Robin says tightly.

"I didn't," Gabe says. *"When I promised to love you till the day I died, I meant it. In less than half an hour my birthday and my life will be over. I will die loving you, and that, my beloved, is a great gift."*

CHAPTER NINE

R obin's body is shaking, and when she speaks, there is a quiver in her splendid voice. *"Stop this Gabe. I want my daughter back."*

"Why? So that one day you can tell her that she no longer meets your needs? For the past six months, I've spent every waking hour trying to figure out what happened between us. I've talked to a colleague of ours in psychiatry who knows you. In fact, he was one of your conquests. He says you have a fear of being abandoned—that's why you always leave other people before they can leave you."

"I will never leave Kali."

"Oh, but you will. Mastery is as necessary to you as oxygen. One day, you'll decide that Kali hasn't turned out quite the way you hoped—she's too tall or too awkward or too dull or just inconvenient. You'll tell her it's time she moved along— that you've found this great boarding school for her. She'll plead with you. She'll promise to change. She'll vow to do whatever it takes to become the person you want her to be. That's when you deliver the coup de grâce and tell her that there is nothing she can do that will make you love her again. There is simply no place for her in your life."

"Gabe, I swear to you…"

"You're not trustworthy, Robin. You've broken your word before." There's no anger in Gabe's voice—just sorrow. *"You offer Kali death by a thousand cuts,"* he says. *"I offer her oblivion. You tell me which is the real act of love?"*

Robin stands so abruptly that her headset is pulled off and clatters noisily onto the desk.

"For God's sake," she says. "Why isn't anybody doing anything?"

Nova's voice over the talkback is urgent. "Help her, Charlie. We'll go to music. Dr. Harris chose Verdi's *Requiem* when we did the pre-interview. We'll play the opening."

"Got it," I say. I turn back to Gabe and our other 150,000 listeners.

"We all need a chance to let our pulse rates slow. Verdi's Requiem—*the choice of our guest expert tonight—should do the job."*

"That will be pleasant," Gabe says. *"Kali and I like Verdi, don't we?"*

I can hear Kali's giggle. So can Robin. She buries her face in her hands. I flip off the button that controls my microphone and move my chair closer to hers.

"I know this is hard," I say, "but try to keep it together. Our producer has been on the phone with the police since we heard Kali's voice. They figure Gabe's using his cell phone, but they're having difficulty tracking his location. You and Gabe were close. Where do you think he would he feel safe with Kali?"

Robin shrugs. "I don't know—his new condo maybe. He gave me the address, but I didn't put it in my book. The hospital will have it." She frowns. "He wouldn't take her there. He knows that's the first place the authorities would look."

"Was there someplace he and Kali liked to go?"

"Alligator Sam's. It's near my house. They have slides, play structures, toys—the kinds of things children enjoy. Gabe said they have a little coffee bar where parents can chat while their children play. Gabe and Kali loved it."

"It's late, Robin. A place for kids would be closed by now."

"Maybe the hospital...? That was always like home to Gabe."

"Which hospital?"

"Lakeshore."

"Okay, I'll pass that along to Nova, but Lakeshore's huge. Where would they even begin?"

"We have codes to alert staff. Code black indicates a personal threat—a hostage situation—a threat of injury or attack. The police will know."

"Good. But, Robin, I have to tell you. I don't think Gabe took Kali there. Hospitals are noisy places, and I didn't pick up any background noise on Gabe's end of the call."

"That's not right," Robin says. "There *was* that bell sound. You noticed it, but I didn't at first. I think it was just one of those noises I was so used to hearing that it barely registered."

"Maybe we'll get lucky and hear it again," I say. "We're going back on the air now. Robin, give Gabe whatever it takes to keep him on the line. Listen for that sound. Try to identify it. It's the only hope we have."

She doesn't move. She seems frozen.

"Are you all right?" I ask.

Robin Harris runs her fingers through her shining auburn hair.

"I'm fine," she says. "I just hate that Gabe is being allowed to control the situation."

I'm dumbfounded.

"This isn't about control," I say. "This is about finding your daughter. If you gave me your daughter's class picture, I couldn't pick her out. All I know about Kali is that she has pajamas that she believes are magic and she knows how to sing 'You Are My Sunshine.' She's a stranger to me, but there is nothing I wouldn't do to keep Gabe Ireland on the line because as long as he's talking to me, he's not telling your daughter that the injection he's about to give her won't hurt a bit."

Robin Harris stares at me, absorbing what I've just said. Then she extends her hands palms up in a gesture of helplessness.

"I don't know how to do this."

I shake my head.

"You are the proverbial riddle wrapped in a mystery inside an enigma," I say. "Dr. Harris, I don't get you. How difficult can it be to make Gabe believe that you love your daughter? That your life will be destroyed if anything happens to her? That a six-year-old child deserves to live?"

She turns, so that once again, I'm confronted with her perfect and distant profile. I'm not a guy who feels he needs to make a point by pounding the table, but tonight, confronted by the lack of comprehension on Dr. Robin Harris's lovely face, I pound the desk.

"Just say the damn words, Robin."

"I can't beg."

Disgust rises in my throat.

"Then fake it," I say. "Because we're back on the air."

CHAPTER TEN

The music fades, and I flip on my microphone.

"My name is Charlie Dowhanuik, and this is 'The World According to Charlie D.' If you've been listening, you know that we have a situation here, so for a while, we're just going to keep our focus on Gabe and Kali. You know what that means. No phone calls. No emails. No texting. No nothing—unless you're sure you can help. So, Gabe, how's it going?"

"Fine. Kali and I are playing Candy Land. Kali just drew a snowflake card. That means she's earned a visit to Queen Frostine's iceberg."

I'm hoping if I keep it light, I can gain some traction.

"So for those of us who've never been to Queen Frostine's iceberg, is that good or bad?" I ask.

Gabe laughs softly.

"Why don't I let you talk to the expert? Kali, my friend Charlie wants to hear about how we play Candy Land. Can you help him out?"

"Sure." Kali's voice has the sweet fizz of soda pop. *"Hi, Charlie,"* she says. *"So what do you want to know?"*

"I need to know pretty much everything." My words to Kali seem to form themselves. *"I think tonight I need to find Candy Land again,"* I say, and the raw yearning in my voice shakes me.

As she explains the game, Kali's voice has the breathless cadences of the schoolyard.

"It's a board game, and it's kind of baby. It's for kids who can't read, and Gabe taught me

69

*to read when I was five. Anyway, it's still fun.
I'll read you the box. It says that Candy Land is
'a sweet little game for sweet little folks.' Gabe
and I each have a little gingerbread person, and
we take our person down the rainbow path,
through the Peppermint Stick forest. The first
one of us who reaches the Candy Castle wins."*

Robin's jaw is tight. Staying in control is
taking its toll.

"Tell her to run."

I shake my head and cover the mike
with my hand.

"Gabe has the hypodermic, Robin."

"Tell her...tell her I love her." Behind
Kali's small voice we hear the bell again.
"There's that sound," Robin says. "Where
have I heard it?"

"Turn on your mike," I say. "Keep Kali
talking. If you hear the bell again, you
might be able to identify it."

"That sounds like fun, Kali," I say.

"It is fun," Kali says. *"I'm caught in the Molasses Swamp now—you're stuck in there until..."*

"Until you draw the red card," Robin says. She's close to tears.

"I didn't think you'd remember the rules," Gabe says. He seems genuinely moved.

"I remember a lot, Gabe." Robin's voice is, as Gabe described it, full of music.

Through the talkback, Nova's voice is tense but excited.

"Dr. Harris is doing exactly what she needs to do. Tell her to ramp it up. If she can make Gabe believe they have a future together, we can save Kali."

CHAPTER ELEVEN

I flick off my mike and touch Robin's arm. "My producer thinks that you're getting through to Gabe. Keep going."

She nods.

"*Gabe, remember the first time we took Kali tobogganing on that big hill over by the ravine? All she wanted to do was race down the hill, but you were worried she'd get hurt. You made her listen to your tobogganing safety rules five times.*"

Gabe laughs softly at the memory.

"*Finally she got bored, leapt onto her sled and just pushed off. When she hit that bump and sailed through the air, I thought my heart would stop.*

"We jumped onto our toboggan and soared after her." Robin looks to me for approval, and I give her what I hope is an encouraging grin. It does the trick. She carries on. *"You and I were such idiots, Gabe. Of course, we hit the same bump Kali did. She was fine, but we nearly broke our backs."*

"Kali was wearing that cap she loved," Gabe says. "The one with the bunny ears. She shook her finger at us and said, 'When you were telling me all that stuff about being careful, weren't you listening?'"

In the background, we hear the sound again. This time I make a connection. I turn off my mike.

"I think it's an elevator bell—the kind elevators in old buildings have. Keep him talking."

Robin takes a deep breath and plunges in again.

"*Then there was that month we spent at Lake Saint Joseph.*"

Gabe's voice is husky with emotion.

"*We made love every morning before Kali woke up. I painted your toenails. The shade was called My Auntie Drinks Chianti—and your toenails were perfect—they looked like small, wet pink petals.*"

"*You and Kali were never out of the water,*" Robin says. "*You taught her how to swim and paddle a canoe. And that sand castle the two of you made—it was a work of art.*"

"*Until the rain came and washed it away. Kali was heartbroken, but you just said, 'Make another one' and went back to that journal article you were writing.*"

Gabe's voice has changed. The joy has given way to a terrible despair.

"*I remember every second of every hour I was with you, Robin. Dante was right: 'There is nothing more painful than remembering happy days in times of sorrow.'*"

Gabe's anguish is a knife in my heart. We've lost him, and that means we've lost Kali. When I meet Robin's eyes, I see a panic that mirrors my own. She turns off her mike.

"It's not working," she says. "Do something."

I grasp at a cliché.

"Time heals all wounds, Gabe," I say. *"You just have to hang on."*

"There's nothing to hang on to, Charlie. That's what I've been trying to tell you. When your show started tonight, you talked about that moment when Eurydice stretches out her arms to Orpheus, but all she can grasp is air. That's the way it will always be for Kali and me. We'll always be reaching for Robin, but we'll never be able to touch her." His voice breaks. *"How could I allow my beautiful Kali to endure that?"*

"She doesn't have to," I say. *"Kali will love other people. Gabe, no one's life hangs on the love of a single person."*

"Your life did," Gabe says gently. *"Over the years, I've often listened to your show. I was listening the night you found out the woman you loved was dead. What was her name again?"*

"Ariel."

"Ariel," he repeats. *"It's a beautiful name—full of light. When you realized you would never touch her again, wouldn't you have given anything for a needle that would end your pain?"*

"That was different," I say. My voice is flat. *"Ariel was...damn it, Gabe. It doesn't matter what Ariel was. She's dead. Kali is alive."*

"And that means terrible things can happen to her. In ten minutes I'll be dead. Nothing will ever hurt me again. What kind of man would I be if I left Kali to face the pain alone?"

Robin reaches for her microphone and clutches it as if it were a lifeline.

"Gabe. I'll come back to you. I promise."

"Don't say another word, Robin. You were never a good liar. I don't want to die knowing that the last words you spoke to me were a lie."

CHAPTER TWELVE

Robin takes off her earphones, folds her arms on the desk and rests her forehead on them. I have no idea how to comfort her. As always when I hit the wall, my gaze travels to the control room. Nova meets my gaze and opens the talkback. The news is not good.

"The police aren't going to find Gabe and Kali," she says. "They're running out of time, and they have no leads. They're focusing on the hospital because, according to Gabriel Ireland's friends, that's where he felt most at home."

"And nothing?" I say.

"Nothing. The hospital has been code black since we learned that Kali was with Dr. Ireland. There are literally hundreds of people looking for them, but that hospital is huge. I'm going to play another Tord Gustavsen tune—give you some time to prepare Robin Harris for the worst."

When she sees that I'm on the talkback, Robin turns her eyes to me. She has the five-mile stare of a person sliding into shock. I don't know how to pull her back. The cool Nordic rhythms of Tord Gustavsen's trio drift through my earphones. Usually the trio's clean, effortless riffs help me to think clearly. Nothing helps tonight. The panic in my chest expands. I'm having trouble breathing.

"There has to be something we can do," I say to Nova.

She shakes her head. "No one's calling. No one's emailing. No one's texting.

Everybody's scared, Charlie. They know that Kali's life is at stake. You asked people to keep the lines open, and that's what they're doing."

"Do you think I should go on-air and make another appeal?"

Nova rubs her eyes. "It can't hurt," she says. "Anything's better than just sitting here listening to the clock tick off the minutes of Kali's life."

I flip on my microphone. Suddenly Nova raises her hand in a halt gesture. "Hold on," she says. "We've got a call."

"Do you want me to take it on-air?"

"Give me a minute to make sure it isn't a hoax."

As she takes the caller's information, Nova's body tenses. Her voice through the talkback is tight with excitement. "This is the real thing. The caller's name is Paulina Terzic. She's a member of the janitorial staff at Lakeshore Hospital. She just came off her shift and tuned us in."

My heart is pounding. "Put her through," I say. I reach for my on-air voice.

"Mrs. Terzic, hello."

"Hello, Charlie. Two things. Have I got time for two things?"

The woman sounds old and kind. Her accent is pronounced.

"Yes, but quickly."

"I understand. One: Dr. Ireland is a good man. Two: he and the little girl are in the old morgue at the hospital. Dr. Ireland and I used to meet there to talk when I was having problems with my grandson. The doctor helped me through a bad time. That's all I have to say." The line goes dead.

Robin bolts upright. "The old morgue. Of course. That sound we've been hearing is the bell on the freight elevator. Tell the police to get in there now!"

The Tord Gustavsen Trio begins another number. Nova has the phone cradled between her ear and shoulder. As she talks, she keys a message on her computer. The words appear on my screen: *Cops heard Mrs. Terzic. They're reluctant to storm the morgue in case Gabe gets spooked and injects Kali. You're their best option. You have to convince Gabe to give himself up and let Kali live.*

Robin has pushed her chair toward me so she can see the screen. When she reads the final sentence aloud, her voice is ragged. Her eyes meet mine. "Please," she says. "It's up to you."

I inhale, lean forward and flip on my microphone. *"We're back. And once again, it's the Gabe and Charlie Show. That means no calls please. No emails. No texts. But prayers and good thoughts are welcome. Is that okay with you, Gabe?"*

Gabe's laugh is edged with sadness. *"Prayers and good thoughts are always welcome,"* he says. *"Now I need your help with something, Charlie. I'm certain the authorities are monitoring your show tonight, but could you remind them that if they force my hand, I'll have to move very quickly and that will frighten Kali?"*

"They're listening, Gabe. But I will remind them to exercise extreme caution. We're all jumpy, but nobody wants to make a mistake."

"Thanks. Right now, we're on schedule. Kali's already reached the Candy Castle. I've lost my last game. Are we having fun, Kali?"

"Yep."

"As long as no one tries to come into our hiding place, we'll keep on having fun." Gabe's pleasant tenor is soothing. *"Kali knows exactly how it's going to be. She's wearing her magic pajamas with the stars that shine in the dark, and...Kali, why don't you tell Mummy what's going to happen?"*

"*Won't that wreck the surprise?*" Kali asks.

When she hears her daughter's voice, Robin bows her head.

"*No,*" Gabe says. "*Because Mummy doesn't need to see us getting the surprise ready. She just needs to see what we've done.*"

"*So it will still be a surprise for her,*" Kali says.

"*It will still be a surprise,*" Gabe agrees.

"*Okay. Mummy when the clock strikes twelve, Gabe's going to turn out the lights so we can see the moons and stars on my pajamas light up in the dark, and we're going to watch them until we fall asleep.*"

"*Oh god!*" Robin's moan is primal—the cry of a trapped animal.

"*Time to get ready,*" Gabe says. "*Let's turn out the lights. Wow, Kali—the moon and stars on your pajamas really do glow in the dark.*"

"*When I move my arms, I can turn the stars into shooting stars,*" Kali says. "*Look Gabe!*"

"That's so beautiful, Kali. Now I'm going to push your sleeve up just a tiny bit. I'll bet the moon and the stars shine even brighter when they get really close together."

Beside me, Robin folds in on herself like a broken doll.

"Oh god," she says. "He's going to do it."

CHAPTER THIRTEEN

Nova is on the phone in the control room. Suddenly her voice comes over the talkback. "Charlie, Danny's on line one. He wants to talk to Gabe."

"Danny's hanging on by a thread himself," I say. "I don't think he's capable of…"

I switch on my microphone.

"Gabe, there's someone who wants to talk to you."

"I'm tired of talking, Charlie D."

"Then just listen. Remember Danny? He called in earlier about his brother's death?"

Gabe doesn't respond. As the silence on the other end of the line grows longer, I wonder if I'm too late.

"Gabe?" I say. He doesn't answer. The next time I call his name, I realize I'm shouting.

"I'm here," he says finally. *"I'll listen to Danny."*

When Danny called in earlier, it was agonizing to hear him speak, but dealing with a problem outside himself seems to free Danny from his demons. The stutter is gone. His voice is heartbreakingly young and urgent, and his message is clear.

"Gabe, you have to listen," he says, *"because I'm probably the only person you'll hear from who's actually killed another person. Even if you only live one second after you kill that little girl, that one second will be too long. You'll die knowing that you changed everything.*

"In physics, we studied this thing called the butterfly effect. It's about how if a butterfly in

the Amazon jungle flaps its wings, that butterfly may eventually change the weather everywhere.

"My brother, Liam, was getting really good with his drums. He might have been a really great drummer. And he was smart—really smart. He might have been the person who found a cure for cancer or stopped global warming. He might have done all kinds of things. I think about that all the time.

"I don't know Kali, but you do. If you kill her, you change everything. Don't do it. Let her have her chance to change the weather."

Robin reaches for her mike.

"Danny's right," she says. "If you do this, we'll never know what Kali could have been— what she could have done. Gabe, she might even have been able to help me."

"You've never needed help."

"I do now," Robin says simply.

Gabe doesn't respond. As the silence continues, I imagine the worst. Gabe pushing up Kali's sleeve, touching her cheek,

injecting the saxitoxin in her small arm.
I look at Robin, and I know from the pain
knifing her face that the movie playing in
her head is the same as the movie playing
in mine.

Suddenly there are voices on Gabe's
end of the line. They are loud and
commanding—the voices of police officers
barking orders. I can hear only fragments
of what they say, but the broken shards
paint a dismal picture.

"He's still alive."

"Stay right where you are, Dr. Ireland."

*"Christ, he must have already killed the girl.
She's not moving."*

Robin begins repeating Kali's name in a
kind of lament.

There's more shouting and then...
Gabe's voice, very calm.

*"Put down your guns. Kali's just sleeping.
Midnight is late for a six-year-old, and this six-
year-old has had a big day. I'm not a threat to*

89

anyone—not even myself. The hypodermic and the saxitoxin are on the other side of the room. Danny was right. Kali deserves her chance to change the weather."

All night, Nova's body has been drawn in on itself with tension. Now she raises her arms in a gesture of relief and triumph. Robin rips off her headset and grabs her coat and briefcase. But instead of moving toward the door, she comes over to me with her hand extended.

"I don't know how to thank you," she says.

"You just did." I take her hand. It's cool and smooth. "Robin, go easy on Gabe," I say.

She nods, but her face is impassive.

It's time to get back to work. I turn on the microphone and find my signature warm-honey voice. *"My name is Charlie Dowhanuik, and you are listening to 'The World According to Charlie D.' It's October thirty-first, the Day of the Dead, and our topic tonight is Death."* I pause. *"So, lessons learned? The big one, I guess, is that nobody knows what happens after we die. That's why what we do here and now matters so much. There's a riddle that's helped me through the night more than once. 'What three words make you sad when you're happy and happy when you're sad?' The answer is 'Nothing lasts forever.'*

"So tonight if you're one of the lucky ones, and your lover or your child is in your arms, hold them close. Cherish the moment. Love is as fragile as luck. If you're alone and your heart is breaking, don't despair. Our grandmothers were right. Tomorrow is another day, and nothing lasts forever. Now, let's let Green Day take us out with that oldie but goody, 'Time of Your Life.'"

CHAPTER FOURTEEN

When Nova and I walk through the front door of CVOX, the hearse is waiting at the curb. Nova looks at me questioningly.

"That's our ride for the evening," I say.

Nova cocks her head and gives me her crooked smile. "Is this a joke?"

"Nope. When I was on my way to work tonight, the driver of that vehicle ran a light and hit me and my Schwinn. My Schwinn didn't make it." I shrug. "I did. I guess it wasn't my night to die."

Nova lifts her face to mine. "Thank God for that," she says. I look into her eyes.

The steadiness in her gaze has anchored me for the past three years.

"I do," I say. I'm surprised at the catch in my voice. And then, another surprise. "Nova, I want to stick around. I want to see what happens next."

The fog has lifted. Above us the red lips and Mick Jagger tongue that form the *O* in the CVOX call letters blaze in the night. Nova slides her arm through mine.

"I've never ridden in a hearse before."

"I guess tonight's your lucky night."

"I know it's my lucky night," she says. For a woman in a caterpillar suit, Nova moves quickly. She reaches up, draws me to her and kisses me.

"Let's go to my place," she says. "Let's see how this story unfolds."

One Fine Day You're Gonna Die is Gail Bowen's second title in the Rapid Reads series. *Love You to Death* also featured late-night radio host Charlie D. Bowen's best-selling mystery series featuring Joanne Kilbourn now numbers an even dozen titles with the recent publication of *The Nesting Dolls*. Winner of both the Arthur Ellis Best Novel Award and the Derrick Murdoch Award for Lifetime Achievement from the Crime Writers of Canada, in 2008 Bowen was named "Canada's Best Mystery Novelist" by *Reader's Digest*.

RAPID READS

The following is an excerpt from
another exciting Rapid Reads novel,
Love You To Death by Gail Bowen.

978-1-55469-262-0 $9.95 pb

Someone is killing some of Charlie D's
favorite listeners.

Charlie D is the host of a successful late-night radio
call-in show that offers supportive advice to troubled
listeners. *Love You to Death* takes place during one
installment of "The World According to Charlie D"—
two hours during which Charlie must discover who
is killing some of the most vulnerable members of
his audience.

CHAPTER ONE

A wise man once said 90 percent of life is just showing up. An hour before midnight, five nights a week, fifty weeks a year, I show up at CVOX radio. Our studios are in a concrete-and-glass box in a strip mall. The box to the left of us sells discount wedding dresses. The box to the right of us rents XXX movies. The box where I work sells talk radio—"ALL TALK/ALL THE TIME." Our call letters are on the roof. The O in CVOX is an open, red-lipped mouth with a tongue that looks like Mick Jagger's.

After I walk under Mick Jagger's tongue, I pass through security, make my way down the hall and slide into a darkened booth. I slip on my headphones and adjust the microphone. I spend the next two hours trying to convince callers that life is worth living. I'm good at my job—so good that sometimes I even convince myself.

My name is Charlie Dowhanuik. But on air, where we can all be who we want to be, I'm known as Charlie D. I was born with my mother's sleepy hazel eyes and clever tongue, my father's easy charm, and a wine-colored birthmark that covers half my face. In a moment of intimacy, the only woman I've ever loved, now, alas, dead, touched my cheek and said, "You look as if you've been dipped in blood."

One of the very few people who don't flinch when they look at my face is Nova ("Proud to Be Swiss") Langenegger.

For nine years, Nova has been the producer of my show, "The World According to Charlie D." She says that when she looks at me she doesn't see my birthmark—all she sees is the major pain in her ass.

Tonight when I walk into the studio, she narrows her eyes at me and taps her watch. It's a humid night and her blond hair is frizzy. She has a zit on the tip of her nose. She's wearing a black maternity T-shirt that says *Believe It or Not, I Used to Be Hot*.

"Don't sell yourself short, Mama Nova," I say. "You're still hot. Those hormones that have been sluicing through your body for nine months give you a very sexy glow."

"That's not a sexy glow," she says. "That's my blood pressure spiking. We're on the air in six minutes. I've been calling and texting you for two hours. Where were you?"

I open my knapsack and hand her a paper bag that glistens with grease from the onion rings inside. "There was a lineup at Fat Boy's," I say.

Nova shakes her head. "You always know what I want." She slips her hand into the bag, extracts an onion ring and takes a bite. Usually this first taste gives her a kid's pleasure, but tonight she chews on it dutifully. It might as well be broccoli. "Charlie, we need to talk," she says. "About Ian Blaise."

"He calls in all the time," I say. "He's doing fine. Seeing a shrink. Back to work part-time. Considering that it's only been six months since his wife and daughters were killed in that car accident, his recovery is a miracle."

Nova has lovely eyes. They're as blue as a northern sky. When she laughs, the skin around them crinkles. It isn't crinkling now. "Ian jumped from the roof of his apartment building Saturday," she says. "He's dead."

I feel as if I've been kicked in the stomach. "He called me at home last week. We talked for over an hour."

Nova frowns. "We've been over this a hundred times. You shouldn't give out your home number. It's dangerous."

"Not as dangerous as being without a person you can call in the small hours," I say tightly. "That's when the ghoulies and ghosties and long-leggedy beasties can drive you over the edge. I remember the feeling well."

"The situation may be more sinister than that, Charlie," Nova says. "This morning someone sent us Ian's obituary. This index card was clipped to it."

Nova hands me the card. It's the kind school kids use when they have to make a speech in class. The message is neatly printed, and I read it aloud. "'Ian Blaise wasn't worth your time, Charlie. None of them are. They're cutting off your oxygen.

I'm going to save you.'" I turn to Nova. "What the hell is this?"

"Well, for starters, it's the third in a series. Last week someone sent us Marcie Zhang's obituary."

"The girl in grade nine who was being bullied," I say. "You didn't tell me she was dead."

"There's a lot I don't tell you," Nova says. She sounds tired. "Anyway, there was a file card attached to the obituary. The message was the same as this one—minus the part about saving you. That's new."

"I don't get it," I say. "Marcie Zhang called in a couple of weeks ago. Remember? She was in great shape. She'd aced her exams. And she had an interview for a job as a junior counselor at a summer camp."

"I remember. I also remember that the last time James Washington called in, he said that he was getting a lot of support from other gay athletes who'd been outed, and he wished he'd gone public sooner."

"James is dead too?"

Nova raises an eyebrow. "Lucky you never read the papers, huh? James died as a result of a hit-and-run a couple of weeks ago. We got the newspaper clipping with the index card attached. Same message— word for word—as the one with Marcie's obituary."

"And you never told me?"

"I didn't connect the dots, Charlie. A fourteen-year-old girl who, until very recently has been deeply disturbed, commits suicide. A professional athlete is killed in a tragic accident. Do you have any idea how much mail we get? How many calls I handle a week? Maybe I wasn't as sharp as I should have been, because I'm preoccupied with this baby. But this morning after I got Ian's obituary—with the extended-play version of the note—I called the police."

I snap. "You called the cops? Nova, you and I have always been on the same side of that particular issue. The police operate in a black-and-white world. Right/ wrong. Guilty/innocent. Sane/Not so much. We've always agreed that life is more complex for our listeners. They tell us things they can't tell anybody else. They have to trust us."

Nova moves so close that her belly is touching mine. Her voice is low and grave. "Charlie, this isn't about a lonely guy who wants you to tell him it's okay to have a cyberskin love doll as his fantasy date. There's a murderer out there. A real murderer—not one of your Goth death groupies. We can't handle this on our own."

I reach over and rub her neck. "Okay, Mama Nova, you win. But over a hundred thousand people listen to our show every night. Where do we start?"

Nova gives my hand a pat and removes it from her neck. "With you, Charlie," she says. "The police want to use our show to flush out the killer."

RAPID READS

The following is an excerpt from
another exciting Rapid Reads novel,
That Dog Won't Hunt by Lou Allin.

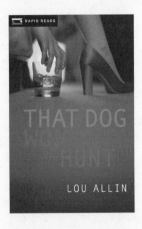

978-1-55469-339-9 $9.95 pb

Sometimes you *can* teach an old dog new
tricks.

Cowboy drifter Rick Cooper is on the run when he
meets Gladys Ryan, an eccentric widow who offers
him a ride in her classic 1970 Mustang. Before long
she convinces him to accompany her and her ancient
golden retriever to Northern Ontario to help run her
late husband's hunting lodge. With the promise of
a share of the season's profits, Rick is happy to go
along. But when Gladys fails to keep her promises at
season's end, everything goes sideways.

CHAPTER ONE

This mirage was made to order. A cherry-red Mustang Mach 1 sat by the side of the road in the Mojave Desert. Its hood was up. Waves of heat rolled off the asphalt like X-rays.

My eyes were sore from squinting. One side of my throat was tickling the other. I took the last swig from a plastic gallon of water I'd bought at Twentynine Palms. Scored a three-pointer against a saguaro. The jug rolled like a tumbleweed. I had been hitching on I-10 east from LA. They might be looking for me on the Interstate, so I took this back road through the Sheephole Mountains toward Vegas. Hadn't seen one damn car in an hour.

Cowboy boots hate asphalt and sand. Fact is, they're not big on walking, period. I hoisted my duffel over my shoulder and headed for the car. The sun beat down like honey. Too dry in the desert for sweat to even bead. Thank god it was April, not July.

"Damn it to hell!" a rough voice yelled. The rear plate read *Ontario*. My mirage was near perfect. Canucks are helpful, and they'll swallow hard-luck stories. Then the hood slammed down.

A wiry woman, barely five feet, with a wide straw hat and sunglasses, puffed on a cigarillo. Female. Three for three. Leading with my "trust me" grin, I approached.

"Where did you come from, cowboy?" she asked, tapping the ash and smiling with a plump red mouth. My boyish look makes women want to mother me.

"A lady in distress?" I took a mock bow, sweeping off my hat. It was battered and stained from a beating I'd rather forget.

Why was she out here alone? Where was she heading? Surely as far as Utah. Canada was way past that.

"You look like a man who knows horses. How about Mustangs?"

Smiling, I trailed a finger over the dust on the door. Hand-buffed and detailed. Someone loved it.

"Let's take a look." Raising the matte black hood with that sexy scoop, I fixed the safety rod.

She took off the hat and fanned herself. The cat's-eye sunglasses made her look like Cher. Throaty laughter said hard years of liquor and tobacco.

"It's fate. Looks like we both took the wrong road. Nothing's come along but a couple of vultures ready to pick my bones." She pointed to a circling bird.

"Shame to waste such pretty bones. Anyways, it's a red hawk. You can tell by the whistle." I reached in and turned the key to watch the gauges. "Not outta gas. Oil's good. Not overheating. What happened to her?"

She shrugged and flipped the plastic tip of the cigarillo toward the sagebrush. "Got herky-jerky at first. Nearly slowed to a stop." She wore a white linen skirt and a floral blouse. Silk scarf around her neck. Like she'd come from a business meeting. Not many women could keep their cool alone in the desert.

I tossed an appreciative glance just to let her know I noticed.

"One thing's sure, we gotta get out of here. Start her up." I moved to the front.

The engine caught right off. But instead of a purr, she sounded like she had the hiccups. Not in the starter then. No back-firing or pinging either. Dirty fuel line?

I signaled to turn off the ignition. Spark-plug connections were good, carburetor flap moved easy. When I removed the distributor cap, I knew what was wrong.

"More gas. But nice and easy. She's talking."

Give Daddy a paper clip, a screwdriver, duct tape and a hose and he'd get anything with wheels moving. From my jeans pocket, I pulled a penknife with a bone handle. Then I exposed the points and scraped.

"Try her now." Listening, I held up a hand, and she read me loud and clear. The engine stopped. I scraped again. "She's hurting but back in business."

The Mustang had enough life to get us to a town. The woman revved the motor.

"You're one damn miracle worker. I'd like to shake your hand, kind sir."

I took out my last handkerchief and cleaned my fingers. "Glad to help."

"I'm Gladys Ryan." She had a firm grip, like she knew what she was doing. It's a western thing. I'm all for being equal. Some women I've seen could ride and rope circles around me. Credit where credit's due, and all that. She wore a real strange ring on her third finger, left hand. Like a cigar band, only colored metal.

"Rick Cooper."

"Gary Cooper. Tall, dark and handsome."

"No relation, ma'am." Mama used to like that dude. Another good sign.

"Looks like we both caught a break. Hop in. You drive," she said.

I tossed my duffel into the trunk beside her set of fancy luggage marked *YSL*. Maybe it was secondhand. Then I eased into the seat and took the leather-wrapped wheel. Daddy always said to keep your hands at ten and two. Looking at the gearshift, I did a double take.

"What the hell's that?"

She gave a little pound to the dash as she laughed. "That's the future, if you get old enough. A steel hip joint."

"I've seen custom, but this beats all." I found first and juiced the gas. I went through all five gears, double-clutching at the top to show off.

Some fierce stink filled the car. "Oh, Christ. Bucky's awake."

"Huh?" I hadn't seen a kid. She was a bit old for that.

"It's my golden retriever in the backseat. You'd never know he was there unless he wakes up for a meal. Then he farts up a storm."

Turns out Bucky was fifteen, old for the breed and on the deaf side. She and her husband had him from a pup. Retrievers weren't my thing. Didn't see the point of them. German shepherds, maybe. Good guard dogs earned their keep.

Her tiny hand reached out to adjust the air conditioner. Blue veins. Not so young then.

Maybe a rough fifty or a prime sixty. That could work in my favor.

"The gear-shift was my late husband George's. He had a hip replacement and a wicked sense of humor."

"Uh-huh." That explained the weird ring. Must've been a cheap bastard.

"I do admire the car. She's choice." Fifty thousand miles on the odometer. Babied big-time for twenty years. "No rust neither. Saw your license. Don't you have salt on the road up there?"

"Kept it covered up inside all winter. Too light in the rear for traction. We used it only for special trips. George had a sister in San Diego. We went down once a year." Her voice took on a sad tone. "I'm… coming back from her funeral."

"Sorry for your loss."

She shrugged and pooched out her lower lip. "She was eighty. When you gotta go…"

"It's not bad to go in California."

"You got that right. How'd you know that trick with the engine?" She reached into the backseat.

"My daddy purely loved Mustangs. The '65 classic, and then the '70 like this one: 351 Cleveland V-8 engine. Same color too. Christmas cars, he called 'em. Red, green, gold stripes." I heard her rummaging around. A metallic clinking. My lips were chapped and I licked them. "Sure would be funny if it was the same one," I said.

"In the movies maybe. George bought this new. Five thousand bucks." She popped the cap off a can of Colt 45 and passed it over.

"That'll hit the spot. Lots of snow up north?" I finished the brew in a couple of gulps.

"We don't all live in igloos like Yanks think. But we plow and shovel plenty of the white stuff." Next came a paper cup and a bottle of Smirnoff. She poured herself a generous slug and toasted me.

RAPID READS

978-1-55469-367-2 $9.95 pb

Can Walter Davis succeed when the odds are stacked against him?

Walter Davis is young, handsome, intelligent and personable. He is also homeless. The medical expenses that came with his mother's unsuccessful battle with cancer have left him destitute. When he meets the girl of his dreams, his situation gets even more complicated. Trying to impress a girlfriend when you have no fixed address proves difficult. And when he's caught in a lie, she shuns his company. Only resilience, ingenuity and his drive to succeed can bring Walter back from the brink of despair.

THE
SPIDER
BITES

MEDORA SALE

978-1-55469-282-8 $9.95 pb

"My name is Rick Montoya. But you can call
me the Spider. Other people do."

When Rick Montoya returns to the city to try to clear
his name, he discovers someone is living in his apartment. Before he can find out who it is, the apartment
house goes up in flames. Was the firebombing meant
for him? Who exactly was killed in the fire? And why?
What was his landlady doing at home in the middle
of the afternoon? The questions mount up, along
with the suspects.

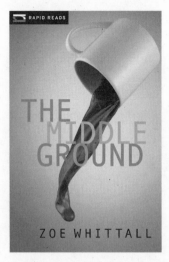

978-1-55469-288-0 $9.95 pb

When everything goes wrong at once, Missy Turner begins to make some unusual choices.

Missy Turner thinks of herself as the most ordinary woman in the world. She has a lot to be thankful for—a great kid, a loving husband, a job she enjoys and the security of living in the small town where she was born. Then one day everything gets turned upside down—she loses her job, catches her husband making out with the neighbor and is briefly taken hostage by a young man who robs the local café. With her world rapidly falling apart, Missy finds herself questioning the certainties she's lived with her whole life.

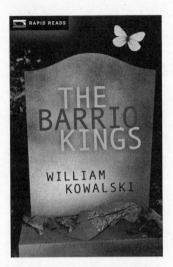

978-1-55469-244-6 $9.95 pb

"Look, man, real life is not always pretty. Sometimes you gotta do hard things. You have to protect what's yours in this life. No one else will do that for you."

Rosario Gomez gave up gang life after his brother was killed in a street fight. Now all he wants to do is finish night school, be a good father and work hard enough at his job at the supermarket to get promoted. But when an old friend from the barrio shows up, Rosario realizes he was fooling himself if he thought he could ignore his violent past.